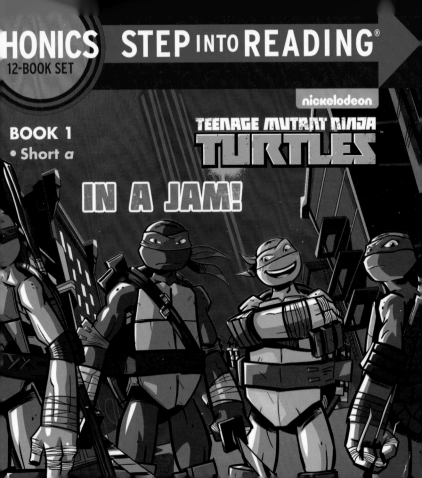

In this book, you will learn the short **a** sound:

bad	can	has	jam
band	fast	jab	ran

You will learn these new sight words:

in   **is**   **the**

You will learn these
Teenage Mutant Ninja Turtles words:

bo **staff**	**Michelangelo**
Donatello	**Raphael**
fight	**robot**
Leonardo	**Turtles**

Leonardo can fight.

Donatello has

a *bo* staff.

He can jab!

Look,

a bad robot!

Michelangelo is

in a jam.

Raphael ran fast.

Raphael can jab

the bad robot!

The Turtles are

one bad band

of brothers!

TEENAGE MUTANT NINJA TURTLES

Learning to Read, Step by Step!

By Jennifer Liberts • Illustrated by Patrick Spaziante

StepIntoReading.com   randomhousekids.com
Box ISBN 978-0-385-38482-7
MANUFACTURED IN CHINA

nick LOVES
READING
nick.com
T#: 306934

nickelodeon

RANDOM HOUSE
StepIntoReading.com

TEENAGE MUTANT NINJA
TURTLES

LEND A HAND

In this book, you will learn the short **e** sound:

get	**lend**	**red**	**tell**
help	**lesson**	**steps**	**yell**

You will learn these new sight words:

are	**him**	**show**
brothers	**not**	**to**

You will learn these
Teenage Mutant Ninja Turtles words:

pizza   **Splinter**

The Turtles

are brothers.

They help each other.

Donatello helps

Michaelangelo.

Leonardo gets a lesson.

Splinter shows him

the steps.

Raphael is mad.

He gets red

in the face.

He yells.

Splinter helps.

He tells Raphael

not to yell.

TEENAGE MUTANT NINJA TURTLES

Learning to Read, Step by Step!

By Jennifer Liberts • Illustrated by Patrick Spaziante

StepIntoReading.com randomhousekids.com
Box ISBN 978-0-385-38482-7
MANUFACTURED IN CHINA

nick LOVES READING
nick.com
T#: 306934

RANDOM HOUSE
StepIntoReading.com

nickelodeon

STEP INTO READING®

nickelodeon

TEENAGE MUTANT NINJA TURTLES

BOOK 3
• Short *i*

BIG CITY

In this book, you will learn the short **i** sound:

big	grin	kick	win
city	is	trip	zip
flip	it	will	

You will learn these new sight words:

again	bad	of	they
away	get	safe	

The Turtles take a trip.

They go to the city.

It is big!

Oh, no!

It is a big bad robot!

It zips!

It flips!

The Turtles will get rid

of the robot!

Raphael kicks!

Michelangelo flips!

The robot zips away!

The Turtles win.

The Turtles grin!
The big city
is safe again.

TEENAGE MUTANT NINJA TURTLES

Learning to Read, Step by Step!

By Jennifer Liberts • Illustrated by Patrick Spaziante

Based on characters created by Peter Laird and Kevin Eastman.
StepIntoReading.com randomhousekids.com
Box ISBN 978-0-385-38482-7
MANUFACTURED IN CHINA

nick LOVES
READING
nick.com
T#: 306934

nickelodeon

RANDOM HOUSE
StepIntoReading.co

PHONICS
2-BOOK SET

STEP INTO READING®

nickelodeon

BOOK 4
Short o

TEENAGE MUTANT NINJA TURTLES

STOP THAT MOB!

In this book, you will learn the short **o** sound:

drop	**jog**	**on**	**rooftop**
fog	**mob**	**plot**	**stop**
job	**not**	**robot**	

You will learn these new sight words:

must	**net**	**see**	**too**	**way**

You will learn this
Teenage Mutant Ninja Turtles word:

Kraang

The Turtles jog.

They jog in the fog.

The Turtles see

Kraang robots!

The robots are

on the rooftops.

The Turtles stop.

They plot a way

to stop the robots.

The robots do not stop!

The Turtles have a job

to do.

They must stop the mob.

They drop a net

on the robots.

TEENAGE MUTANT NINJA TURTLES

Learning to Read, Step by Step!

By Jennifer Liberts • Illustrated by Patrick Spaziante

StepIntoReading.com   randomhousekids.com
Box ISBN 978-0-385-38482-7
MANUFACTURED IN CHINA

nick LOVES
READING

nick.com
T#: 306934

nickelodeon

RANDOM HOUSE
StepIntoReading.com

In this book, you will learn the short **u** sound:

cut	fun	must	trust
duck	jump	run	

You will learn these blends:

ck	st	tr

You will learn these new sight words:

a	fast	left	win
down	first	right	

The Turtles must train.

It is fun.

First,

the Turtles must run.

They run fast.

They run and run.

Uh-oh!

The Turtles see robots.

They must duck down.

The Turtles do not

trust robots.

Leonardo jumps up!

Michelangelo jumps up!

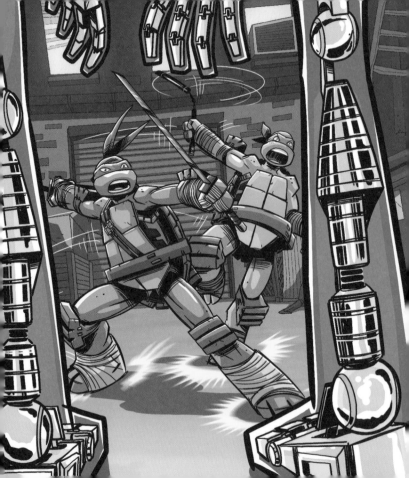

The robots cut left!

The robots cut right!

They make a run for it.

The Turtles win!

TEENAGE MUTANT NINJA TURTLES

Learning to Read, Step by Step!

By Jennifer Liberts • Illustrated by Patrick Spaziante

StepIntoReading.com   randomhousekids.com
Box ISBN 978-0-385-38482-7
MANUFACTURED IN CHINA

RANDOM HOUSE
StepIntoReading.co

ONICS
2-BOOK SET

STEP INTO READING®

nickelodeon

BOOK 6
• Review of Short
Vowel Sounds
and Blends

In this book, you will review short vowel sounds:

bad	flip	help	lots	spin
can	fun	in	must	stop
city	grin	jump	not	win
fast	have	kick	run	

You will learn these letter blends:

ck   sp   st

You will learn this new sight word:

guys

You will review these
Teenage Mutant Ninja Turtles words:

Donatello   **Michelangelo**   **Turtles**
Leonardo   **Raphael**

Michelangelo can flip!

Donatello can kick!

Raphael can jump!

Leonardo can spin!

The Turtles have

lots of fun.

There are bad guys

in the city.

The Turtles are fast.

They can stop them!

Michelangelo needs help.

Donatello must run fast!

The Turtles grin.

The bad guys

did not win.

TEENAGE MUTANT NINJA TURTLES

Learning to Read, Step by Step!

By Jennifer Liberts • Illustrated by Patrick Spaziante

StepIntoReading.com   randomhousekids.com

Box ISBN 978-0-385-38482-7
MANUFACTURED IN CHINA

nick LOVES
READING

nick.com
T#: 306934

RANDOM HOUSE
StepIntoReading.co

In this book, you will learn the long **a** sound:

April	**chase**	**plates**	**taste**
bake	**day**	**safe**	**tasty**
birthday	**make**	**shake**	**way**
cake	**okay**	**take**	

You will learn these blends:

ch   **gr**   **pl**   **sh**

You will learn this new sight word:

great

It is a great day!

It is April's birthday!

Donatello bakes

a birthday cake.

He makes a tasty cake

for April.

The cake tastes great!

The Turtles take the cake

to April.

They get chased

on the way.

The van shakes!

Oh, no!

The cake!

The cake is okay!

The Turtles are safe.

They eat cake

on plates.

It tastes great!

Happy birthday, April!

TEENAGE MUTANT NINJA TURTLES

Learning to Read, Step by Step!

By Jennifer Liberts • Illustrated by Patrick Spaziante

nick.com
T#: 306934

RANDOM HOUSE
StepIntoReading.co

nickelodeon

ONICS
-BOOK SET
STEP INTO READING®
nickelodeon
TEENAGE MUTANT NINJA
TURTLES
OOK 8
Long e
Blends
MEAN STREETS

In this book, you will learn the long **e** sound:

beat	**keep**	**meet**	**speed**
green	**mean**	**need**	**street**

You will learn these blends:

cr   **gr**   **sp**   **st**

You will learn this new sight word:

creatures

You will learn this
Teenage Mutant Ninja Turtles word:

Snakeweed

The Turtles are green.

They are speedy!

The Turtles are

on the streets.

They keep

the streets safe.

The bad guy is green.

The bad guy

is Snakeweed!

He is mean.

The Turtles need

to beat him.

The Turtles need

to speed.

They speed

to catch Snakeweed.

The Turtles keep

the streets free

of mean creatures!

TEENAGE MUTANT NINJA TURTLES

Learning to Read, Step by Step!

By Jennifer Liberts • Illustrated by Patrick Spaziante

StepIntoReading.com   randomhousekids.com
Box ISBN 978-0-385-38482-7
MANUFACTURED IN CHINA

nick LOVES READING
nick.com
T#: 306934

RANDOM HOUSE
StepIntoReading.co

nickelodeon

STEP INTO READING®

nickelodeon

TEENAGE MUTANT NINJA
TURTLES

FIND THAT GOO!

In this book, you will learn the long **i** sound:

drive   **hide**   **like**   **time**
find   **light**   **night**

You will learn these blends:

dr   **gh**

You will learn these new sight words:

go   **guy**   **no**
goo   **last**   **out**

It is night.

The Turtles like

to go out at night.

The lights are on.

It is time for pizza!

The Turtles like pizza.

Oh, no!

The pizza guy

finds some goo.

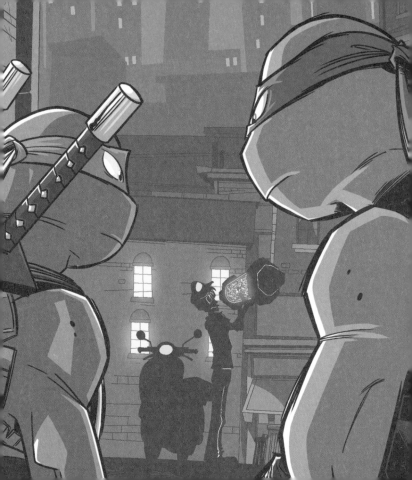

The Turtles must get

the goo in time!

It is time to drive!

The Turtles find the goo!

They hide it.

TEENAGE MUTANT NINJA TURTLES

Learning to Read, Step by Step!

By Jennifer Liberts • Illustrated by Patrick Spaziante

StepIntoReading.com   randomhousekids.com
Box ISBN 978-0-385-38482-7
MANUFACTURED IN CHINA

nick LOVES
READING

nick.com
T#: 306934

RANDOM HOUSE
StepIntoReading.co

nickelodeon

TEENAGE MUTANT NINJA TURTLES

BOOK 10
• Long *o*
• Blends

ROBOT FOES

In this book, you will learn the long **o** sound:

clone	**home**	**oh**	**robot**
foe	**no**	**okay**	**throw**
go	**obey**	**only**	**zone**

You will learn these blends:

cl   **nt**   **sp**   **th**

You will learn these new sight words:

does	**there**	**want**
many	**them**	

Michelangelo wants

to go out.

Splinter says no.

Michelangelo goes!

He does not obey.

Michelangelo sees a robot.

It is okay.

There is only one robot.

Oh, no!

Clones!

There are so many robots!

It is a robot zone.

Michelangelo throws

the robots.

He knocks them over.

Michelangelo goes home.

Home is a safe zone!

TEENAGE MUTANT NINJA TURTLES

Learning to Read, Step by Step!

By Jennifer Liberts • Illustrated by Patrick Spaziante

StepIntoReading.com   randomhousekids.com
Box ISBN 978-0-385-38482-7
MANUFACTURED IN CHINA

nick LOVES
READING

nick.com
T#: 306934

RANDOM HOUSE
StepIntoReading.co

nickelodeon

nickelodeon

TEENAGE MUTANT NINJA
TURTLES™

BOOK 11
• Long *u* and *oo*
• Blends

SUPER
DUDES

In this book, you will learn the long **u** and **oo** sounds:

blue	food	new	true	use
dude	glue	super	tube	

You will learn these blends:

bl	ing	th
in	sk	tr

You will learn these new sight words:

can	invent	wear
favorite	thing	

You will learn these
Teenage Mutant Ninja Turtles words:

mask   ninja

The Turtles

are super dudes.

Leonardo wears

a blue mask.

Donatello uses

glue and tubes.

He invents new things!

Raphael is a strong dude.

Pizza is Michelangelo's

favorite food!

The Turtles are true ninjas.

TEENAGE MUTANT NINJA TURTLES

Learning to Read, Step by Step!

By Jennifer Liberts • Illustrated by Patrick Spaziante

StepIntoReading.com   randomhousekids.com
Box ISBN 978-0-385-38482-7
MANUFACTURED IN CHINA

nick LOVES READING
nick.com
T#: 306934

nickelodeon

RANDOM HOUSE
StepIntoReading.com

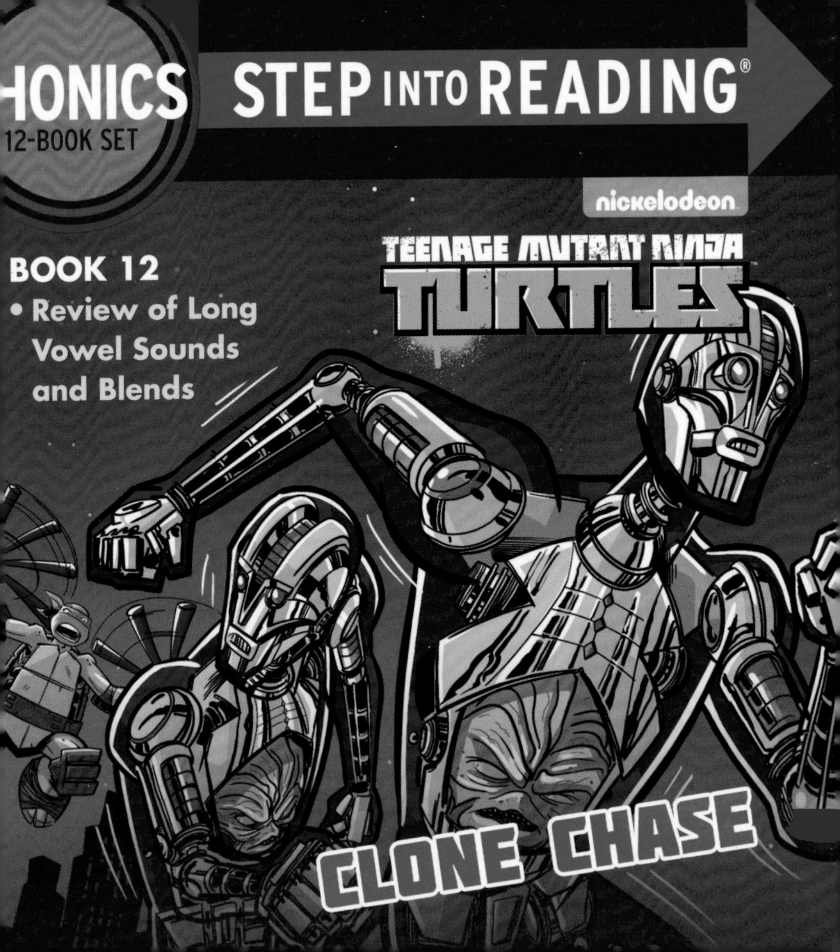

HONICS
12-BOOK SET
STEP INTO READING®
nickelodeon
BOOK 12
• Review of Long Vowel Sounds and Blends
TEENAGE MUTANT NINJA
TURTLES™
CLONE CHASE

In this book, you will review long vowel sounds:

blue	find	home	time
chase	five	need	use
clone	green	rescue	
drive	hide	speed	
dude	high	super	

You will review these blends:

bl	cl	gh	sp
ch	gr	sc	th

A blue robot

finds green goo!

The Turtles need

to get the goo

in time.

There is not much time.

The Turtles use

super speed!

The Turtles drive!

The blue robot

has five clones!

The robots hide

the green goo.

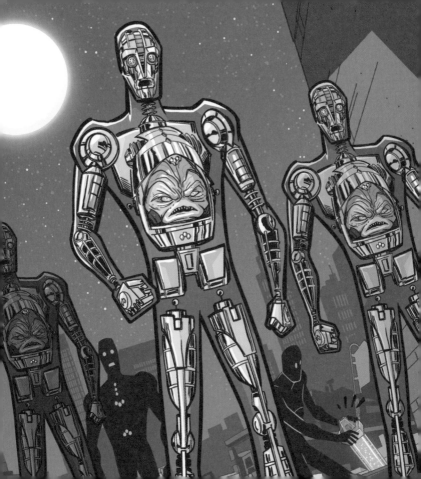

The Turtles get there

in time!

The Turtles

rescue the goo.

They are super dudes!

The Turtles chase

the robot clones.

The robots go home.

Time for high threes!

TEENAGE MUTANT NINJA TURTLES

Learning to Read, Step by Step!

By Jennifer Liberts • Illustrated by Patrick Spaziante

StepIntoReading.com randomhousekids.com
Box ISBN 978-0-385-38482-7
MANUFACTURED IN CHINA

RANDOM HOUSE
StepIntoReading.com

nickelodeon